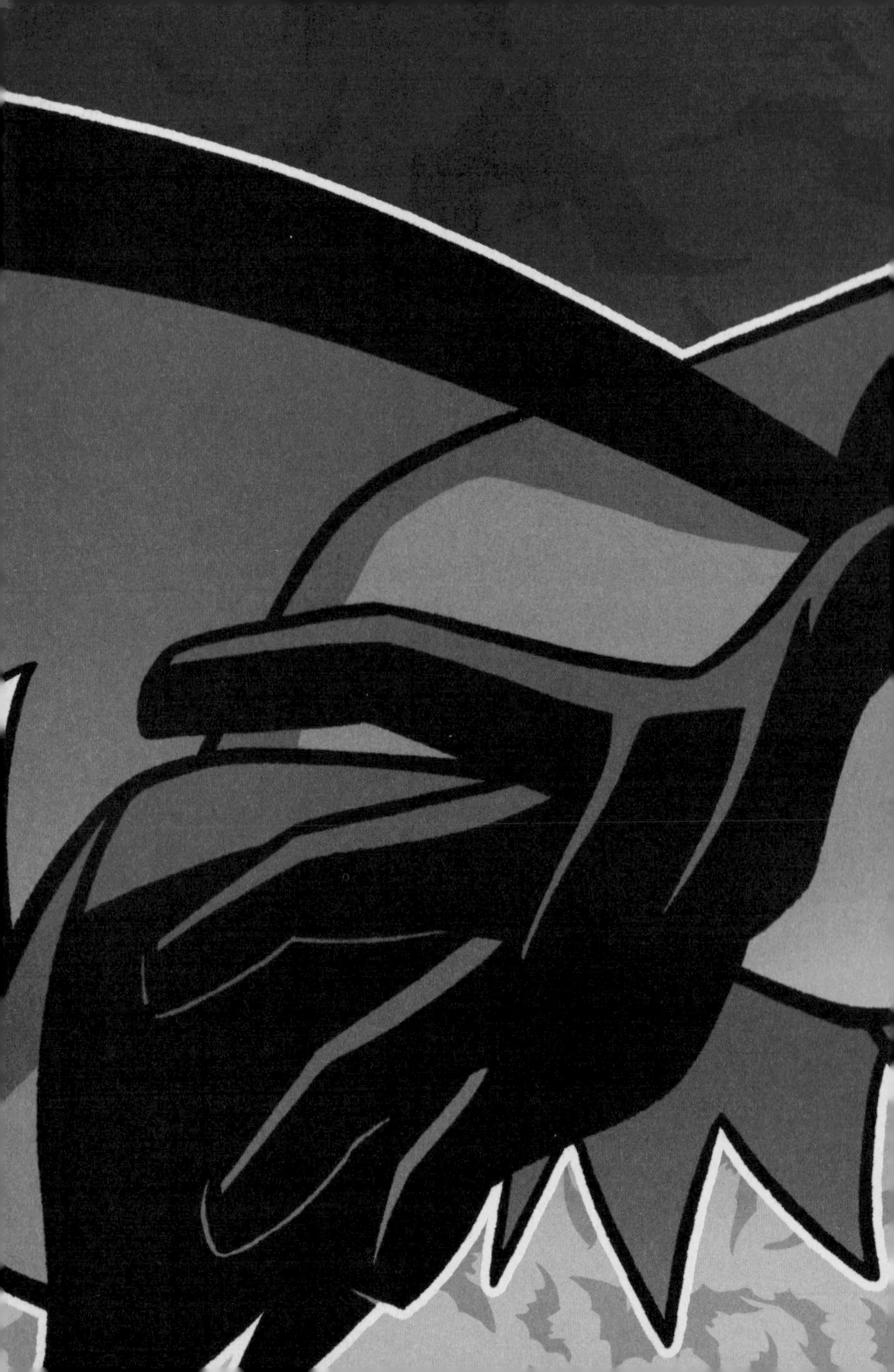

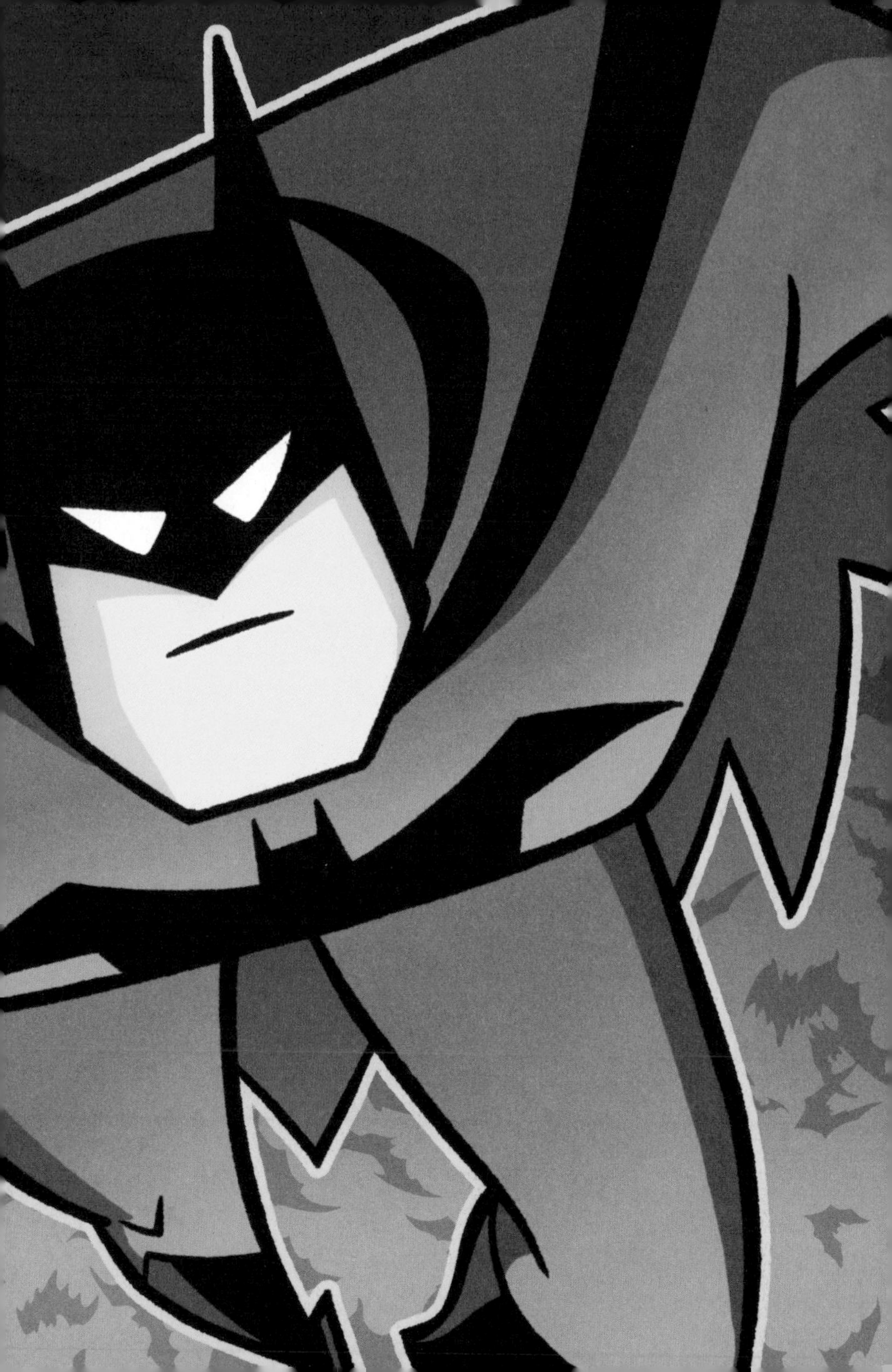

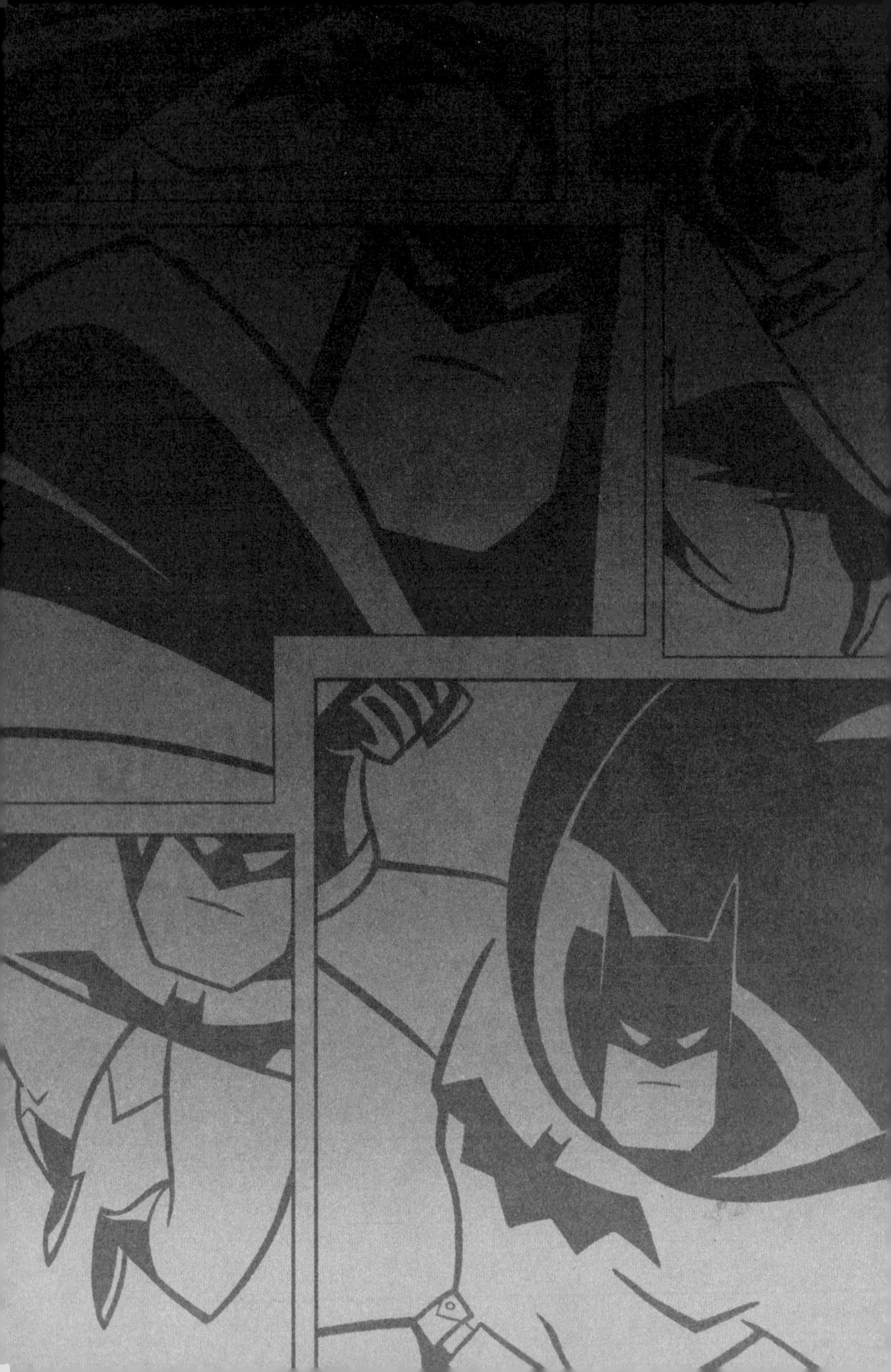

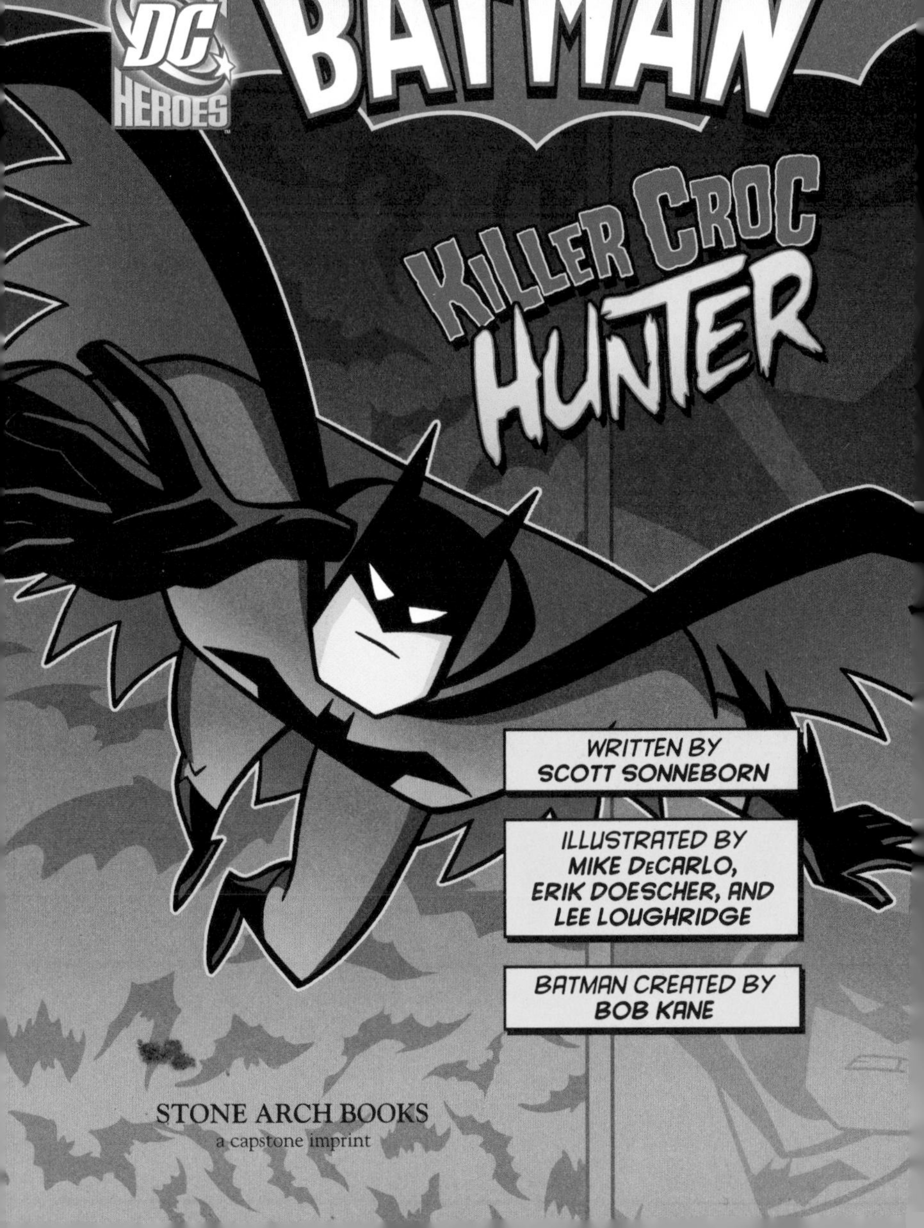

SUPER DC HEROES

BATMAN

KILLER CROC HUNTER

WRITTEN BY
SCOTT SONNEBORN

ILLUSTRATED BY
MIKE DeCARLO,
ERIK DOESCHER, AND
LEE LOUGHRIDGE

BATMAN CREATED BY
BOB KANE

STONE ARCH BOOKS
a capstone imprint

Published by Stone Arch Books in 2010
A Capstone Imprint
151 Good Counsel Drive, P.O. Box 669
Mankato, Minnesota 56002
www.capstonepub.com

Library of Congress Cataloging-in-Publication Data

Sonneborn, Scott.
  Killer Croc hunter / by Scott Sonneborn ; illustrated by Erik Doescher ;
illustrated by Mike DeCarlo ; illustrated by Lee Loughridge.
    p. cm. -- (DC super heroes. Batman)
  ISBN 978-1-4342-1876-6 (library binding) -- ISBN 978-1-4342-2258-9 (pbk.)
  [1. Superheroes--Fiction.] I. Doescher, Erik, ill. II. De Carlo, Mike, ill. III.
Loughridge, Lee, ill. IV. Title.
  PZ7.S6982Ki 2010
  [Fic]--dc22

                                                2009029088

Summary: As a pro wrestler, Killer Croc bullied his opponents inside the
ring. As a cutthroat criminal, this ferocious freak forces his competition out
of town. Next on his hoodlum hit list is Kite Man, but the second-rate super-
villain isn't leaving Gotham without a fight. He's partnering with Batman, the
World's Greatest Detective, to wrangle up the Killer Croc and put him down
for the count.

Art Director: Bob Lentz
Designer: Brann Garvey
Production Specialist: Michelle Biedscheid

Printed in the United States of America in Stevens Point, Wisconsin.
092009
005619WZS10

TABLE OF CONTENTS

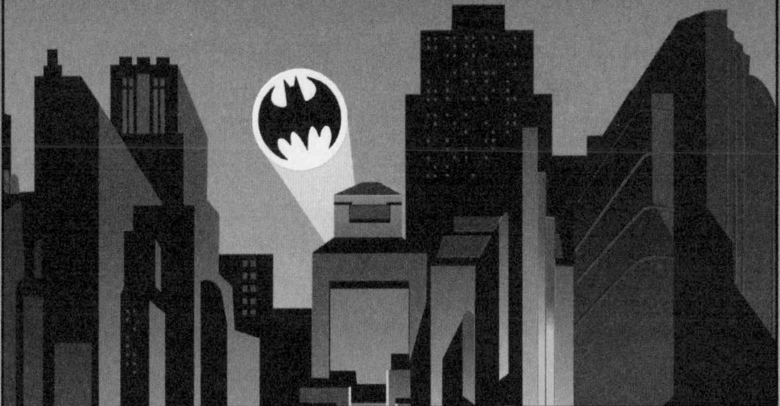

CHAPTER 1

THE PENNY PLUNDERER

The Penny Plunderer smiled.

He'd just finished robbing Gotham City's Rare Coin Vault. The crime had taken him months of sleepless nights to plan. During that time, he'd pinched his pennies — eating nothing but donuts and frozen peas.

It had all been worth it.

Lugging a huge sack, the Plunderer made his way down the vault's front steps. The bag held 50 pounds of rare pennies worth twice their weight in gold.

At the bottom of the steps, the Plunderer stopped to take one last look at the vault. The Penny Plunderer had never been happier. He closed his eyes, enjoying the moment.

He never saw the punch coming.

POW! Killer Croc brought his scaly fist down on top of the Penny Plunderer's head. The Plunderer collapsed in a heap, down for the count.

Croc was very big and very strong. He stood more than seven feet tall, and every inch of him was covered with hard, green scales. He looked down at the Plunderer and smiled a toothy grin.

"This dummy works months on this heist," Croc said, laughing. "And I get all the money with just one punch!"

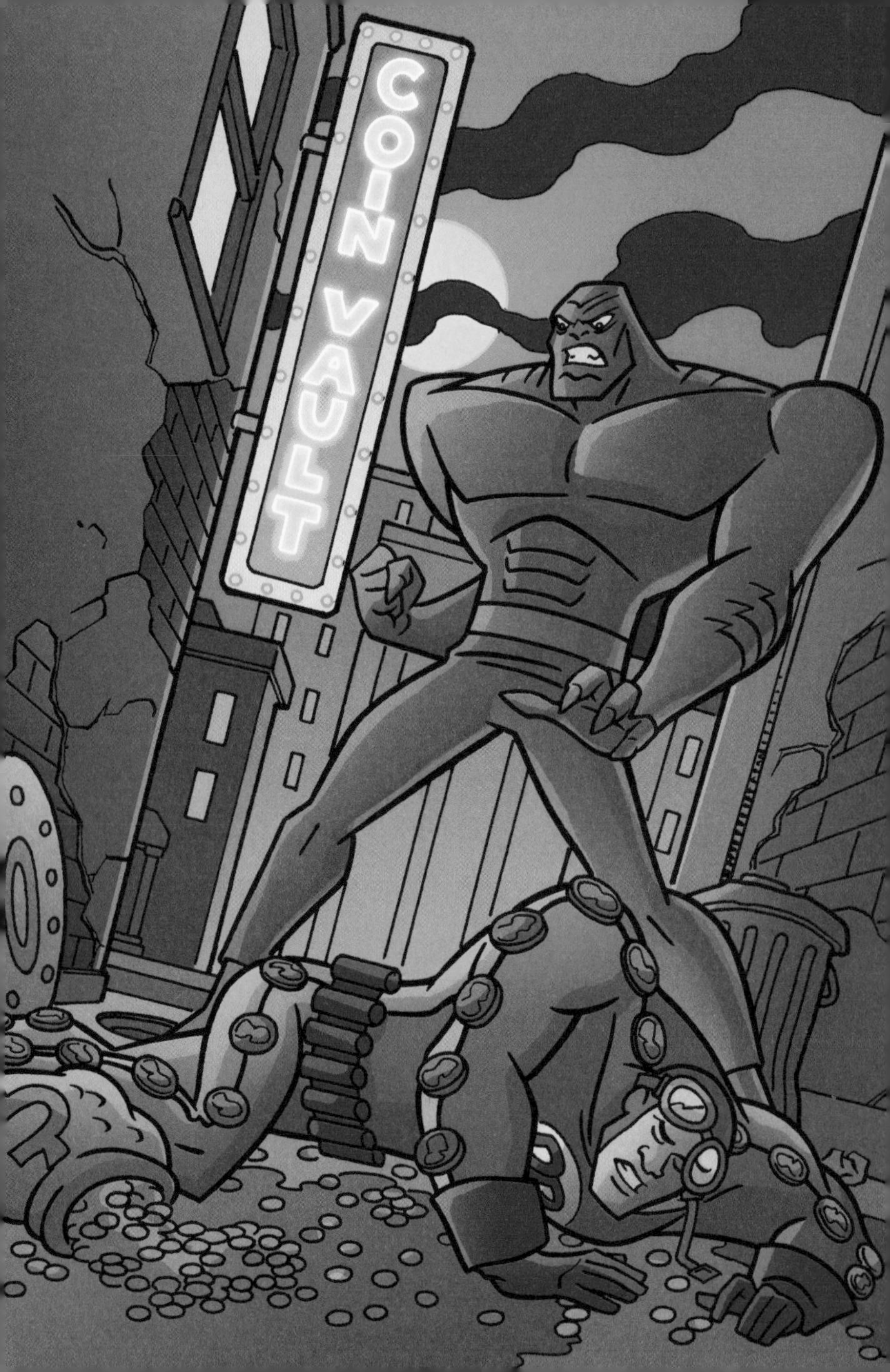
COIN VAULT

Killer Croc bent down and picked up the sack of million-dollar pennies. "Easy money," he said to himself, snorting.

SMASH! Croc tore open the manhole cover nearby. He jumped down, disappearing into the sewers.

Ten minutes later, the Batmobile rolled to a stop in an alley. Batman leaped from the car, fired his grapnel gun, and soared up to the Rare Coin Vault rooftop.

He looked down on the scene below. The Gotham police were already there. They had handcuffed the Penny Plunderer.

"Why are you arresting me?" cried the Plunderer. "I was robbed!"

"After *you* robbed the vault," the police officer reminded him. "When we catch the guy who robbed you, we'll arrest him too."

If you catch him, thought Batman.

For the past week, Killer Croc had been on a spree. He'd discovered a new way to get rich. He let other villains do the stealing. Then he took their loot by force.

Croc wasn't dumb enough to steal from the Joker or Clayface or any of Gotham's super-villains. He robbed crooks like the Penny Plunderer. The Plunderer was a villain, but there wasn't anything super about him. In fact, he was kind of pathetic.

Batman had a name for crooks like the Plunderer. He called them "silly villains."

Croc had robbed several silly villains. In fact, there were just two Croc hadn't robbed yet — Kite Man and Mr. Polka-Dot.

Find them, thought Batman, *and I'll find Killer Croc.*

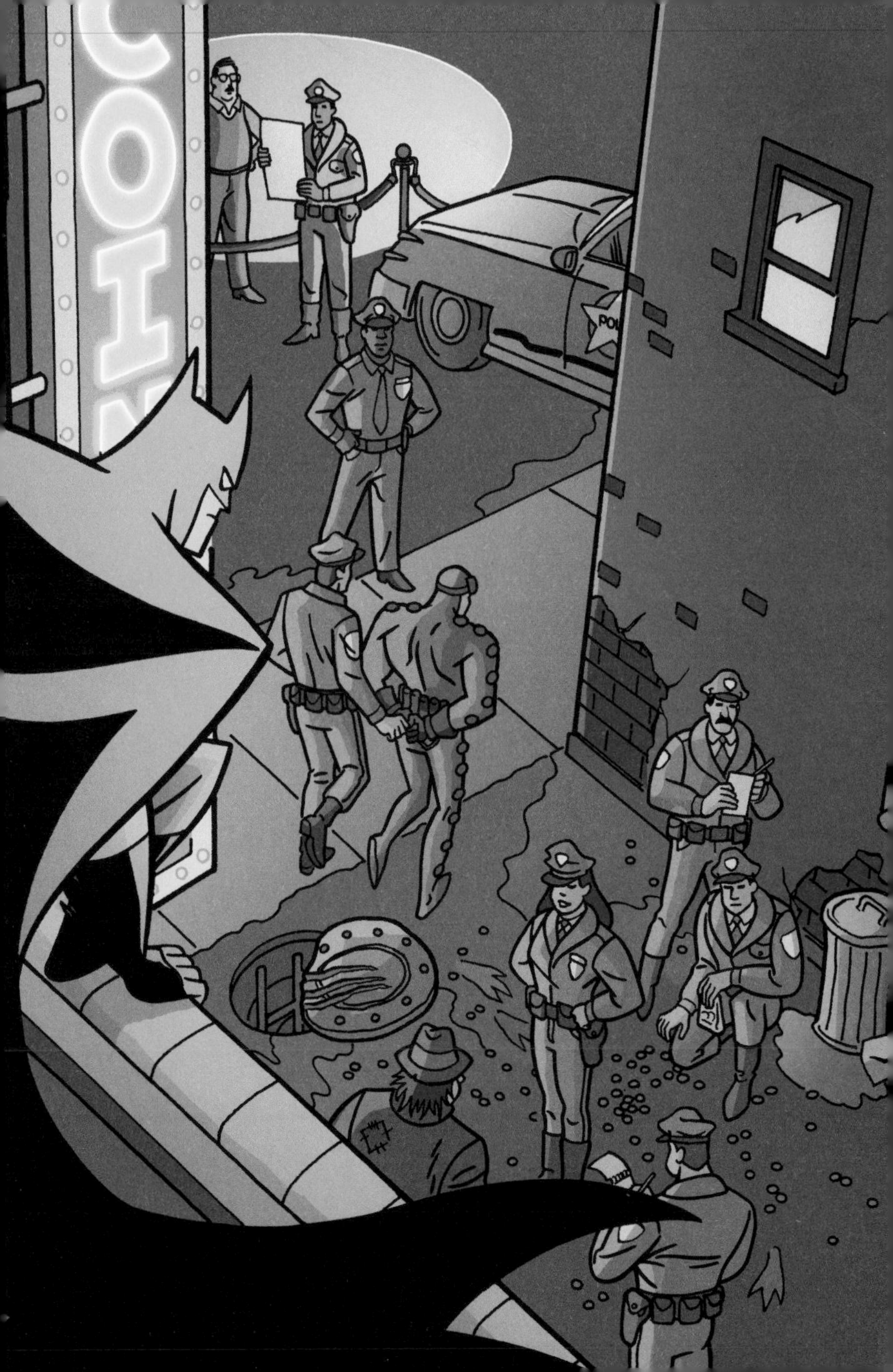

CHAPTER 2

KITE MAN

Batman returned to the Batmobile and accessed the computers in the Batcave. He downloaded the files on Killer Croc, Kite Man, and Mr. Polka-Dot. Kite Man's file came through first, followed by Croc's.

Croc's file was ten times the size of Kite Man's, which made sense. Croc was one of the worst, most feared villains in all of Gotham City. Killer Croc had the strength and speed — not to mention the claws and the teeth — of a crocodile. He was also just as fierce.

Kite Man, on the other hand, was a villain who liked kites. *You have got to be kidding me,* Batman thought, frowning.

* * *

Gotham City's Museum Mile was lined with tall marble buildings. The Museum of Space Technology was nine stories tall. The Warfare Museum was fourteen.

The Kite Museum occupied the top floor of a run-down office building. Its "security system" was a single rusty lock.

Kite Man had stolen the key for the rear entrance door a few days ago. He was just about to insert the key into the lock.

The door to the Kite Museum suddenly burst open.

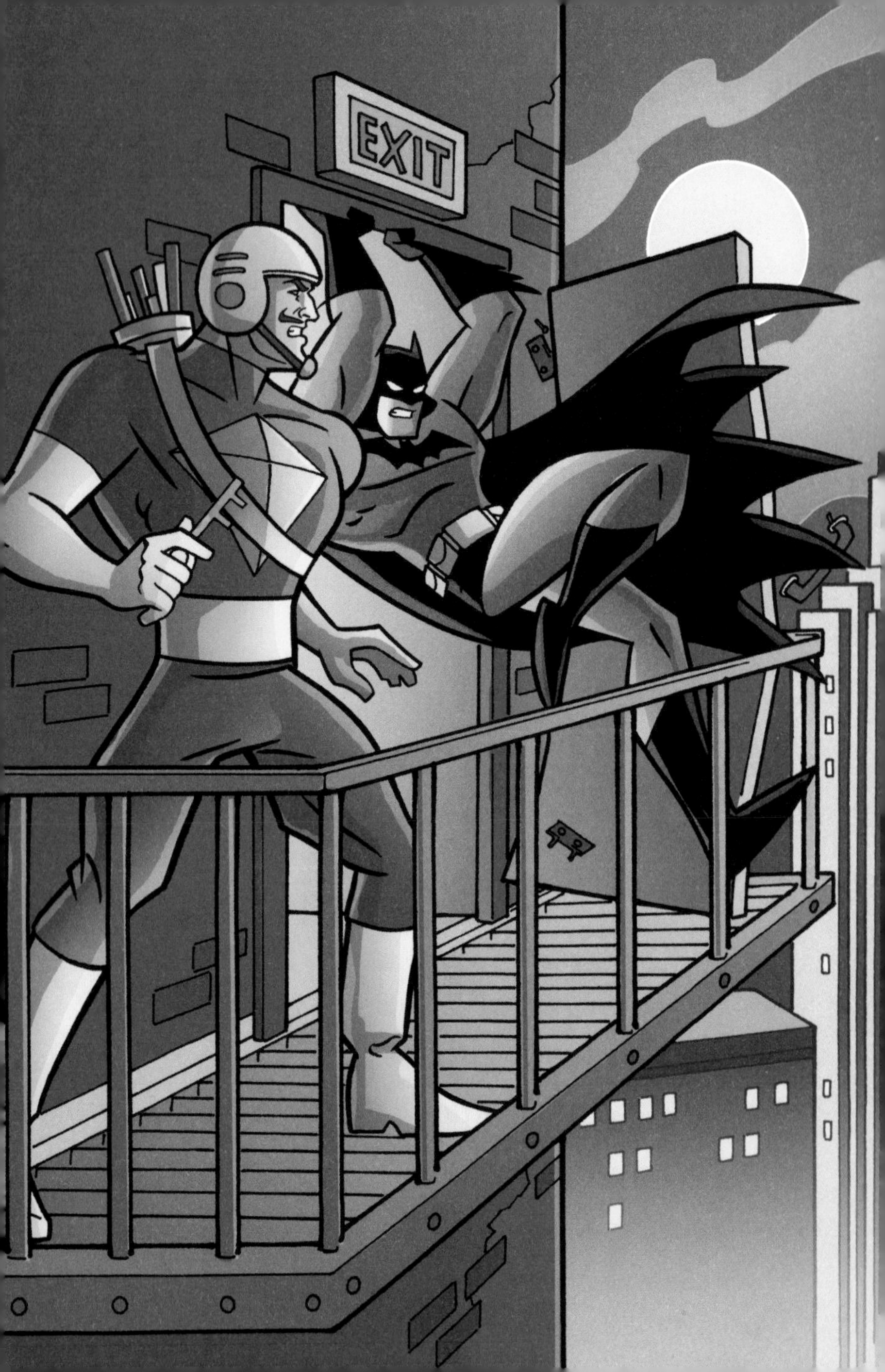
EXIT

"Come in," said Batman, standing in the open doorway. "We need to talk."

"How'd you get in there?" exclaimed Kite Man. "Seriously, I'd really like to know how you did it. Are you going to help me steal the museum's kites?"

"That's not why I'm here," growled Batman, shaking his head.

"Fine. I wouldn't expect a do-gooder like you to help a master criminal like me!" replied Kite Man. "Prepare to feel the righteous fury of my kites!"

Kite Man reached for his quiver of kites. In a split second, Batman's Batarang flew through the air and smacked the silly villain's hand away.

"Ow!" yelped Kite Man. "That hurt!"

"Quiet!" shouted Batman. "I'm trying to help you. Killer Croc has been robbing minor-league crooks. In the past two days, he's robbed the Clock, the Calculator, and the Penny Plunderer. I think that you're next."

Kite Man couldn't believe what he was hearing. He frowned at Batman.

"Oh, go fly a kite!" he snorted. "Me? Minor league? I'm nothing like the Clock, Penny Plunderer, or the Calculator for that matter. Those guys are silly. There's nothing silly about me. I mean, I'm here to rob the Kite Museum!"

"I didn't come here to discuss your career," said Batman. He was quickly losing his patience. "I'm trying to protect you from Croc."

"*You* protect *me*? That's a good one," said Kite Man. "In case you hadn't noticed, I'm the one holding the kites!"

Kite Man got up in Batman's face. "By the way, if I'm so 'minor league,'" continued Kite Man, "how come you've never caught me?"

Batman and Kite Man stepped inside the museum. The Dark Knight leaned over the much shorter Kite Man. Kite Man stuck out his chest in response, a golden kite stretching across his costume.

"It was never worth my time," replied the Dark Knight. "The police always seemed to do it without any trouble."

"They just got lucky last time," said Kite Man. "Okay, and the time before that . . . and, well, yes, the time before that too."

Batman was getting angry. He didn't have time to argue with a small-time crook who thought he was a big deal. The Dark Knight started to say just that, when he was suddenly interrupted.

A scaly green menace smashed through the window!

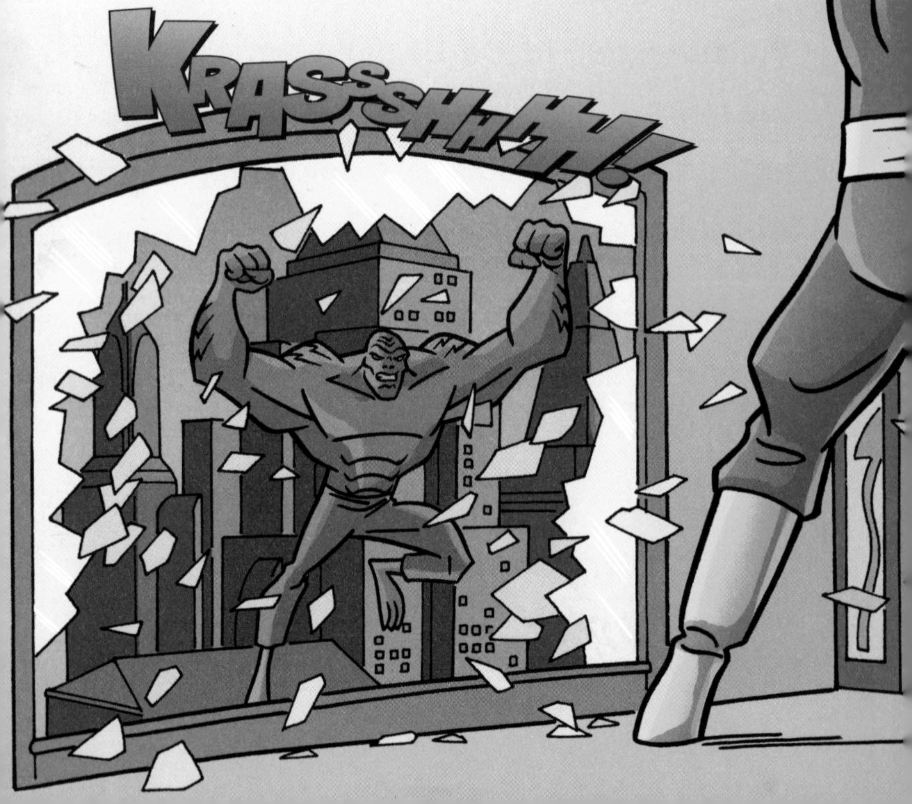
KRASSSHHHH!

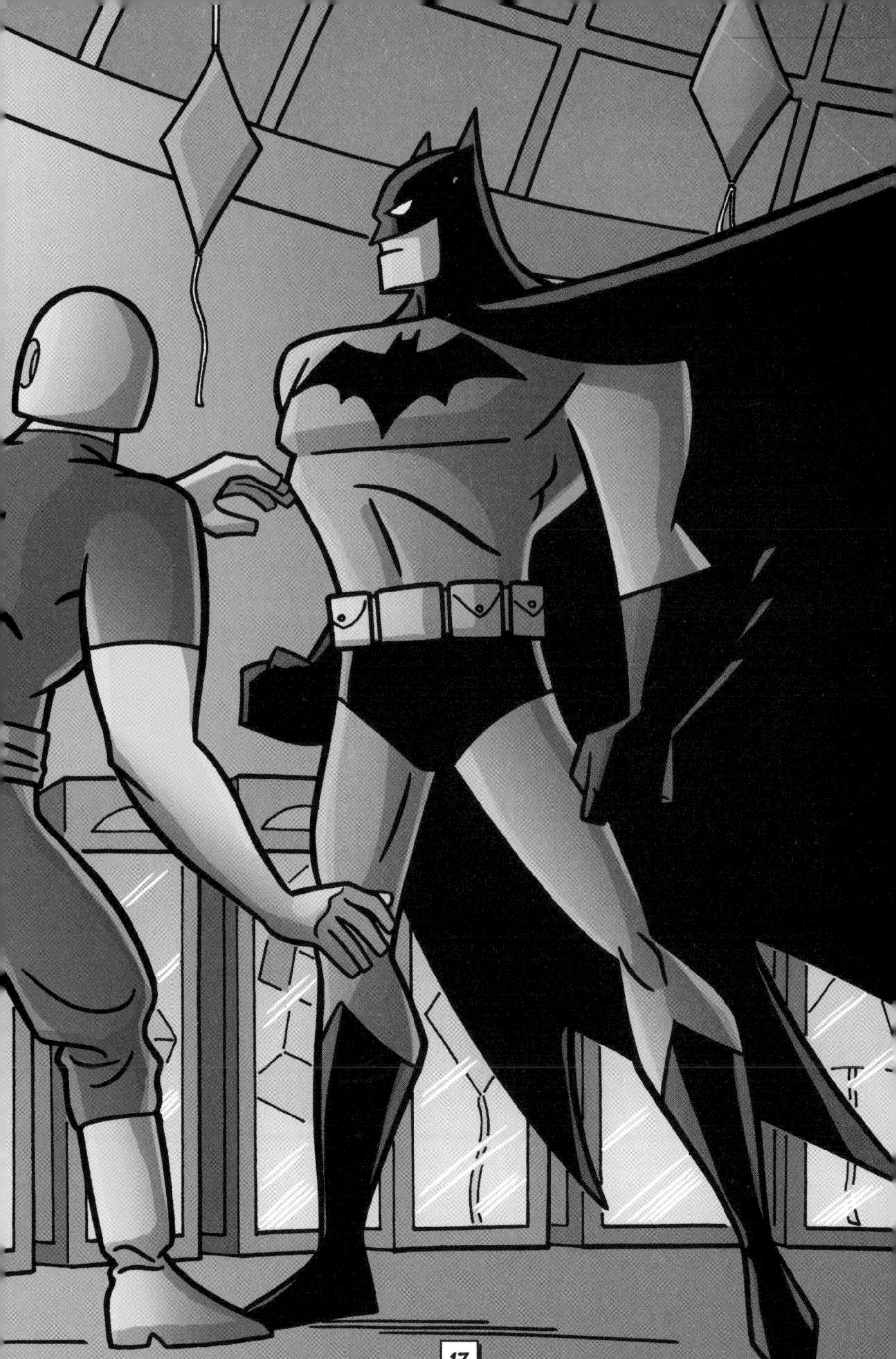

CHAPTER 3

KILLER CROC BURSTS IN!

Killer Croc's enormous figure lunged through the shattered glass.

"Get behind me!" Batman yelled to Kite Man.

"I can take care of myself," replied Kite Man. "I've got kites!"

Kite Man held up two kites. Batman quickly shoved Kite Man out into the hall and slammed the door behind him. Then he turned to face Croc as the scaly giant lumbered toward him.

"I don't know what you're doing here Batman, but I've got no beef with you," said Croc. "In fact, you should be thanking me. I'm doing your job by clobbering crooks."

"I stop criminals," said Batman. "You rob them. That makes you a criminal, too."

Batman crouched low, ready for a fight. "Which means I have to stop you," he said.

"Good luck," said Croc with a laugh. He raised his two meaty fists. "I'm twice as big as you are!"

That wasn't quite true. Croc was actually three times Batman's size. He was fast, too. Before Batman could stop him, Croc ripped an enormous display cabinet off the wall.

"Hurrggh!" Croc groaned as he heaved it at Batman.

Antique kites flew off the 1000-pound display as it zoomed toward Batman. He ducked, and the display smashed into the door that led to the hall. **CRASH!!**

Kite Man stepped into the room through the broken door. "You should really be more careful where you shove people," Kite Man scolded Batman. "You could have broken one of my kites!"

Instead of answering, Batman dropped to the floor. **WHOOOOSH!** Croc's punch just missed him.

"Hello there, Croc," said Kite Man. "We've never actually met. I'm Kite Man, another super-villain here in Gotham."

Kite Man put out his hand. Croc couldn't shake it — both of his hands were busy lifting Batman off the ground.

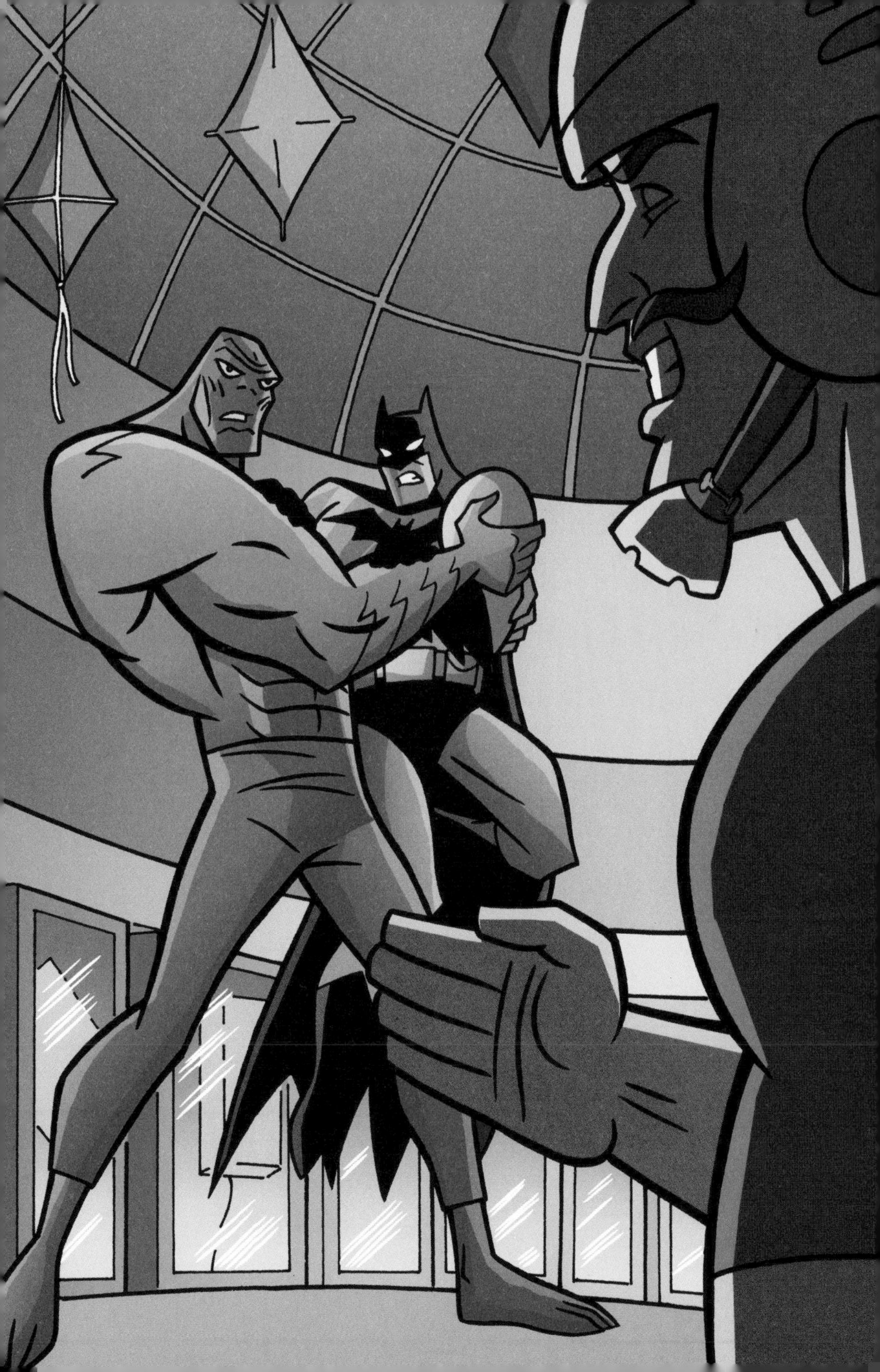

"I can see you're busy, so I'll get right to the point," continued Kite Man. "Before Batman so rudely shoved me aside, I was hoping to ask you something."

Croc's only reply was a roar as he swung a fist at Batman.

"If you can believe it, Batman thinks I'm on the list of 'silly villains' you're trying to rob," said Kite Man. "And don't you try to deny it, Batman," he added, turning to the Dark Knight.

Batman didn't deny anything. He was too busy dodging Croc's claws.

"So just to settle this once and for all," said Kite Man. "You don't think I'm silly, do you?"

"Silly? Nah," said Croc as he slammed Batman to the ground. SMASH!

"Thank you," said Kite Man, beaming. "See, Batman? I told you!"

Pinned under Croc's weight, Batman couldn't answer.

"The other guy left on my list is Mr. Polka-Dot. *He* is silly," continued Croc as he turned to Kite Man. "*You* are ridiculous."

With Croc distracted by Kite Man, Batman took the opportunity to attack. He put everything he had into one big punch. **KA-POW!** The blow connected right in the giant villain's green stomach. The punch would have sent anyone else to the ground. Croc just burped. Then he brought both fists down on Batman's shoulders. Batman collapsed to the floor with a grunt.

Croc stood up and poked Batman with a scaly foot. Batman didn't move.

The big brute smiled and turned back to Kite Man.

"Like I was saying, you're ridiculous. You're trying to rob a museum full of kites!" Croc said, laughing. "You're not even stealing something worth taking from you!"

Croc headed for the door. Kite Man got in front of him and pointed to one of the old kites on the wall.

"You're the one who's ridiculous," huffed Kite Man, "if you can't recognize the value of a vintage 1957 Airfoil kite!"

Croc paused, raising an eyebrow. "How much is it worth?" he asked, interested.

"At least seven dollars!" said Kite Man proudly.

Croc just shook his head. He shoved Kite Man aside and continued toward the door.

Kite Man's eyes filled with fury. "It's one thing to mock me, but I won't stand here and let you insult a 1957 Airfoil!" he roared. "Prepare to taste the awesome power of kites!"

Kite Man charged into battle. He yanked a kite from his quiver and tried to fly it at Croc. **FLAP!** It bounced off the ceiling of the museum and crashed to the floor.

"Um, looks like this room's a little too small to fly my kites," said Kite Man. "Do you mind if we take this outside?"

"Sure!" laughed Croc. He picked up Kite Man and held him out the window.

"Urk!" Kite Man yelped as Croc dangled him over the side of the building. Kite Man looked down. It was at least a hundred feet to the sidewalk below.

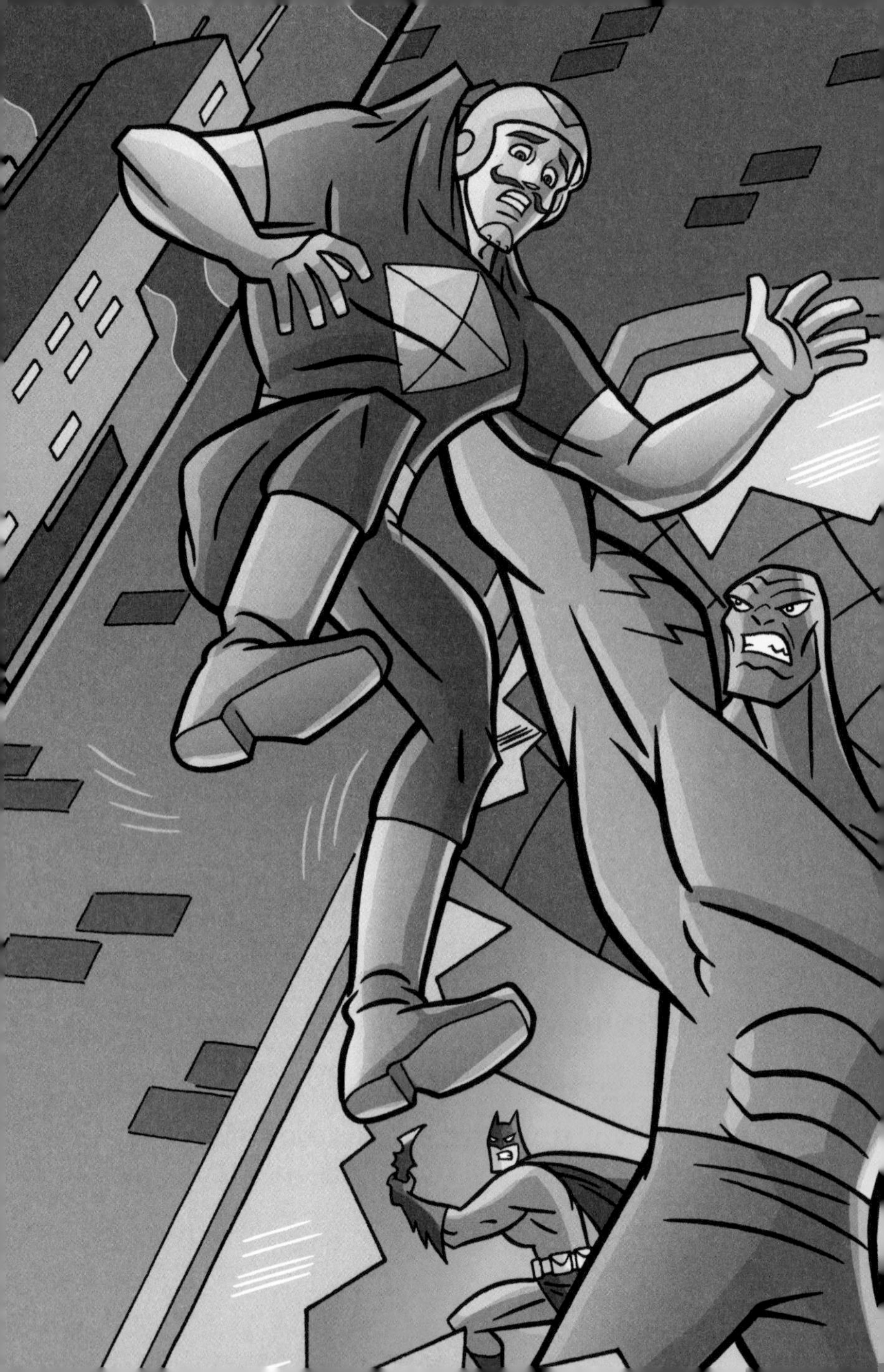

"Let's see if Kite Man can fly!" laughed Croc as he released his grip.

Just as Kite Man started to fall, a Batarang shot out and wrapped a rope around Kite Man's legs. Croc turned to see Batman stagger to his feet. Batman held the other end of the rope attached to the Batarang in his hand.

"I've wasted enough time here," shouted Croc. "Hopefully Mr. Polka-Dot is stealing something worthwhile!"

Croc leaped out of the window. He crashed down through the sidewalk below, and then dived into the sewers.

Batman couldn't follow. He was the only thing keeping Kite Man from falling to his death. Batman pulled hard and yanked Kite Man back into the room.

"Find some place to hide until I take care of Croc," said Batman. "He's way out of your league."

"Hey, you're the one who let him get away!" huffed Kite Man. "I had everything under control!"

Batman didn't reply. He was already out the window and on the hunt for Killer Croc.

CHAPTER 4

MR. POLKA-DOT

As Batman drove through the streets of Gotham, he looked over at the Batmobile's sonar. It sent sound waves bouncing down through the sewers, hunting for Croc.

Every ping on the sonar was a sound wave bouncing back to the Batmobile to reveal the results of its search. The answer was always the same.

Nothing.

Batman turned off the sonar and turned on his police radio scanner. There were reports of trouble at Arkham Asylum, a robbery at the Eastside Bakery, and a break-in at Gotham City's Department of Transportation.

Batman slammed on the brakes and spun the Batmobile around. *The Department of Transportation is also known by its initials: D.O.T.,* thought Batman. *If there's trouble at the "DOT," odds are Mr. Polka-Dot's involved. And where Mr. Polka-Dot is, I'll find Croc!*

Moments later, the Batmobile slowed to a stop next to a chain-link fence. Batman leaped out of the Batmobile and hid behind a car in the parking lot. The huge lot was filled with garbage trucks and snowplows.

Suddenly, Batman heard something heading his way. **WHOOOOSH!**

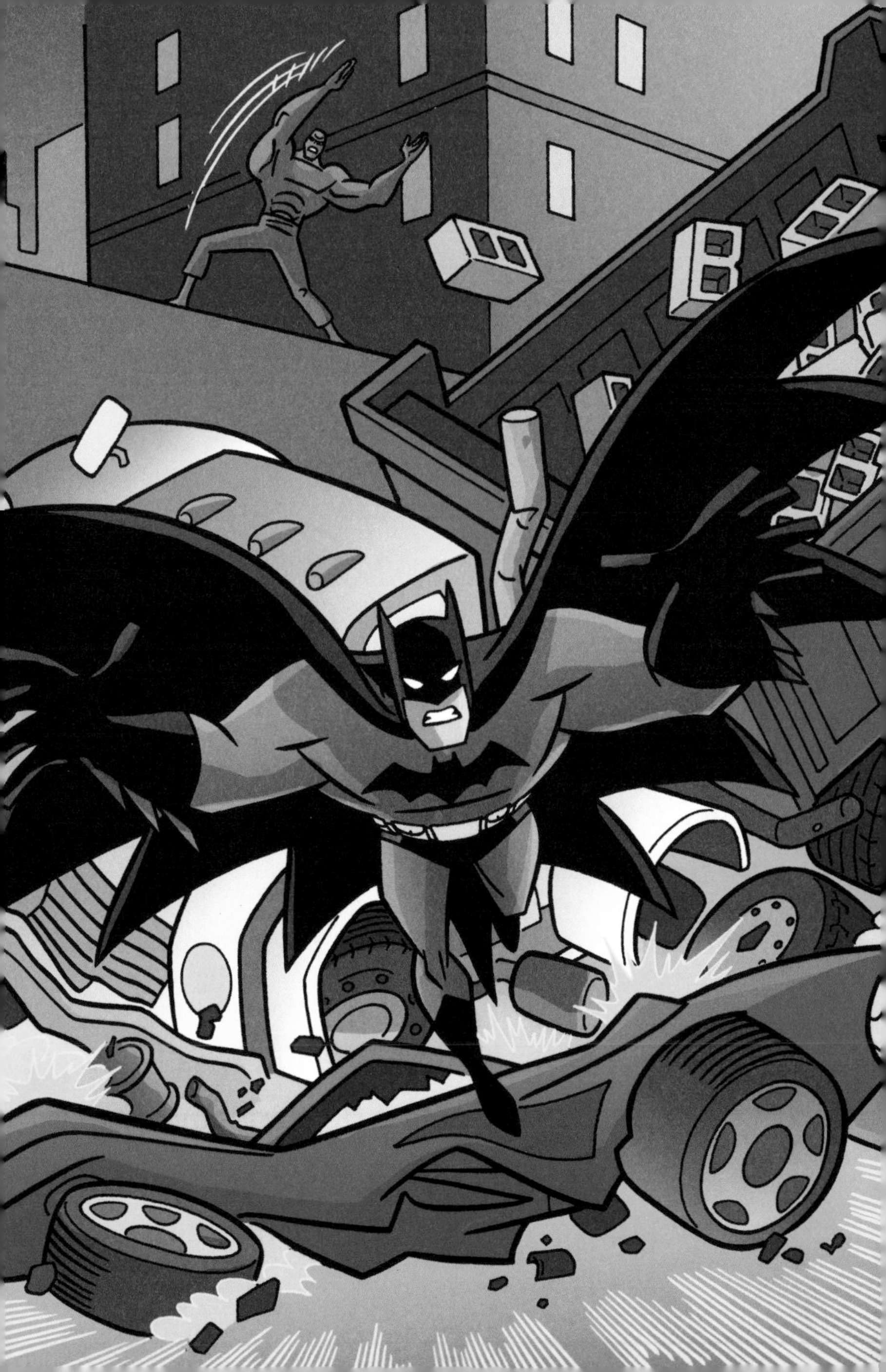

CRUNCH! A garbage truck fell out of the sky and smashed the car Batman was hiding behind! He had leaped out of the way just as the truck landed. The car crumpled like paper under the weight of the giant garbage truck.

"Aw, I missed!" yelled Croc from the DOT parking lot. The scaly villain lifted a nearby street sweeper above his head.

The Dark Knight didn't wait for him to throw it. Batman leaped to safety. He landed between two telephone repair trucks and ducked into the darkness.

The full moon was the only light in the lot. The tall city vehicles threw long shadows over the ground. Batman used the dark to his advantage. He crept quickly through the maze of cars and trucks. *I have to find Croc before he finds me,* he thought.

Like a bat, he ignored his eyes and used his ears. He heard his own breathing, the traffic on the street outside, and the soft padding of feet on concrete.

Croc's feet, Batman thought.

Slipping from shadow to shadow, Batman followed the sound through the maze of vehicles. There was Croc. The monstrous villain was only a hundred yards away, but he didn't see Batman hiding in the dark.

Silently, Batman unclipped a special Batarang from his Utility Belt. It was loaded with enough tranquilizer to send a rhino on a power nap. If Batman were lucky, it would be enough to stun Croc.

This won't be easy, thought Batman. *Croc's scaly hide is as tough as armor.*

There was only one weak spot between the scales on Croc's chest. Batman's Batarang had to hit Croc in that exact spot for the tranquilizer to work.

Batman knew he'd only get one chance. He aimed the Batarang and threw it as hard as he could. It flew out of the darkness toward Croc.

Just then, a loud voice yelled out, "Hey! Batman!" Croc looked up and saw the Batarang. *TWANNNGG!* He knocked it away before it could hit him.

Batman turned to see who had shouted his name. A bald man in a polka-dotted costume ran up to him. "I never thought I'd say this, but am I glad to see you, Batman!" said Mr. Polka-Dot, panting. "I was just minding my own business, robbing this place, when Croc —"

WHAM! Batman knocked Mr. Polka-Dot out. *The police will pick him up when they get here,* thought Batman. *I don't have time to deal with this crook right now.*

As Batman pulled another tranquilizer Batarang from his Utility Belt, he saw Croc sink his claw-like fingers into the metal hood of a garbage truck. "Urgh!" grunted Croc, as he lifted up the truck and threw it at Batman like he was tossing a football.

Batman dived out of the way. The truck barely missed him. **SMASH!** It hit a car, sending metal and glass flying everywhere.

"Hurruggh!" cried Croc. Two more cars flew at Batman. He ducked, and then jumped into a nearby snowplow. Batman put the massive vehicle into gear. The Dark Knight roared toward Croc at 60 miles per hour. **VROOOOM!!**

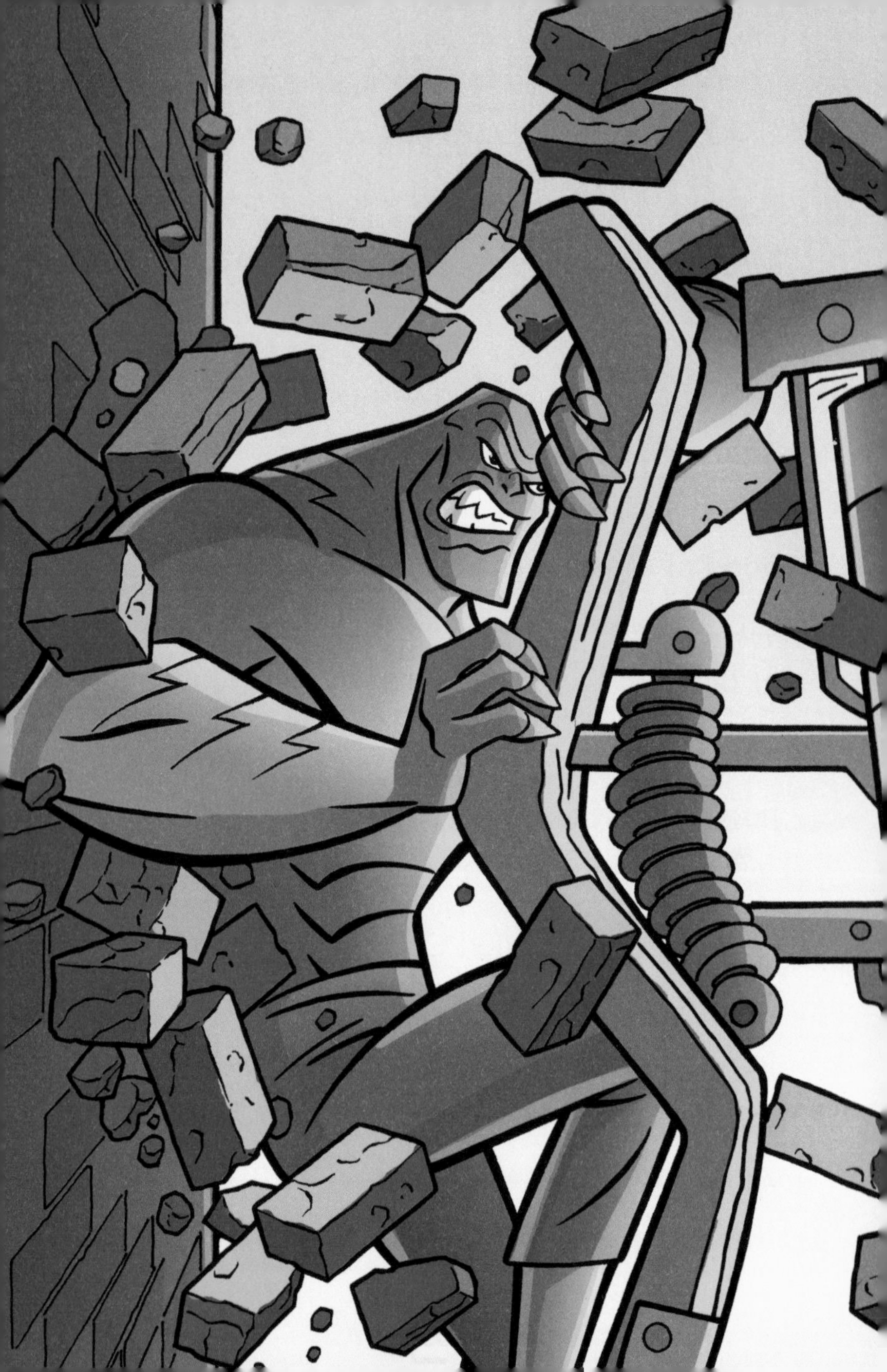

The snowplow crushed Croc int

Batman quickly pulled himself to his feet. *Where did Croc go?* Suddenly, a cold claw grabbed Batman by his neck.

"That kind of hurt," Croc growled. He held Batman five feet off the ground. Batman struggled to break free, but it was no use. Batman was just a man. He was no match for Croc's superhuman strength.

Batman ran through his escape options. There were none. There was only one good thing about the situation.

It couldn't get any worse.

Just then, a shadow fell over Batman. He looked up and realized he had been wrong.

Things *were* about to get worse.

TWO AGAINST CROC

Batman saw that the shadow belonged to Kite Man. He was standing on top of a parked city bus.

"Well, well," said Kite Man. "Look who needs Kite Man's help now!"

Batman struggled, but Croc just tightened his grip.

"You don't deserve it after the rude way you treated me, but I'm going to save you, Batman!" Kite Man boasted. "Just to teach Croc a lesson."

Kite Man quickly unrolled a giant red kite. He expertly guided it into the air, and flew it in the moonlight. He aimed the kite right at Killer Croc.

The big villain tried to duck, but it was too late. The massive red kite hit him right in the chest. It crumpled into a pile of paper and balsa wood.

"Uh-oh," said Kite Man.

"You thought a stupid kite would stop me?" laughed Croc. "It's made of paper and wood! What did you think would happen?"

"Uh . . ." was Kite Man's only answer.

Still holding Batman in one hand, Croc used the other to yank hard on the kite string, pulling Kite Man down from his perch.

"Woooah!" cried Kite Man as he was yanked off of the bus.

Croc caught the airborne criminal in his free hand. "You two have wasted enough of my time tonight!" he roared.

Killer Croc threw Batman and Kite Man into an empty cement mixer. *CRUNCH!* *CRUNCH!* Croc mashed it shut around them, trapping them inside.

Batman pounded on the metal walls of the mixer. They were a foot thick and made of solid steel.

Suddenly, police sirens wailed in the distance. "Wonderful. Now I've got to hurry up and finish robbing this place before the police get here," muttered Croc.

Inside the cement mixer, Batman reached into his Utility Belt.

He pulled out a mini-torch and sparked its flame to life. **POOF!**

Using the torch, Batman began to cut a hole in the mixer's thick wall.

Batman turned to look at Kite Man. "Croc will be gone before the police get here," said Batman. "We have to take him down now."

Batman returned his focus to burning a hole with his torch. "I think I know how to stop him," Batman said, "but I'm going to need your help, Kite Man."

"Oh, just leave me alone, will you?" said Kite Man. He sat down and crossed his arms in a huff. "Croc was right. I'm just a silly villain. I must have been an idiot to think my stupid kites could do anything useful."

Batman finished cutting through the cement mixer. "Actually," the Dark Knight said, smiling, "I think a kite is exactly what is going to bring Croc down."

*   *   *

On the other side of the Department of Transportation parking lot, Croc lifted a car over his head. He grinned and threw it into the back of a giant dump truck. **WHAM!** It landed on top of five other vehicles Croc had tossed in there.

"Now this is how you steal cars!" Croc said, ripping the doors off the dump truck. Croc climbed behind the truck's steering wheel and started to turn the key.

THUD! Batman swung in through the side window, slamming into Croc with his feet.

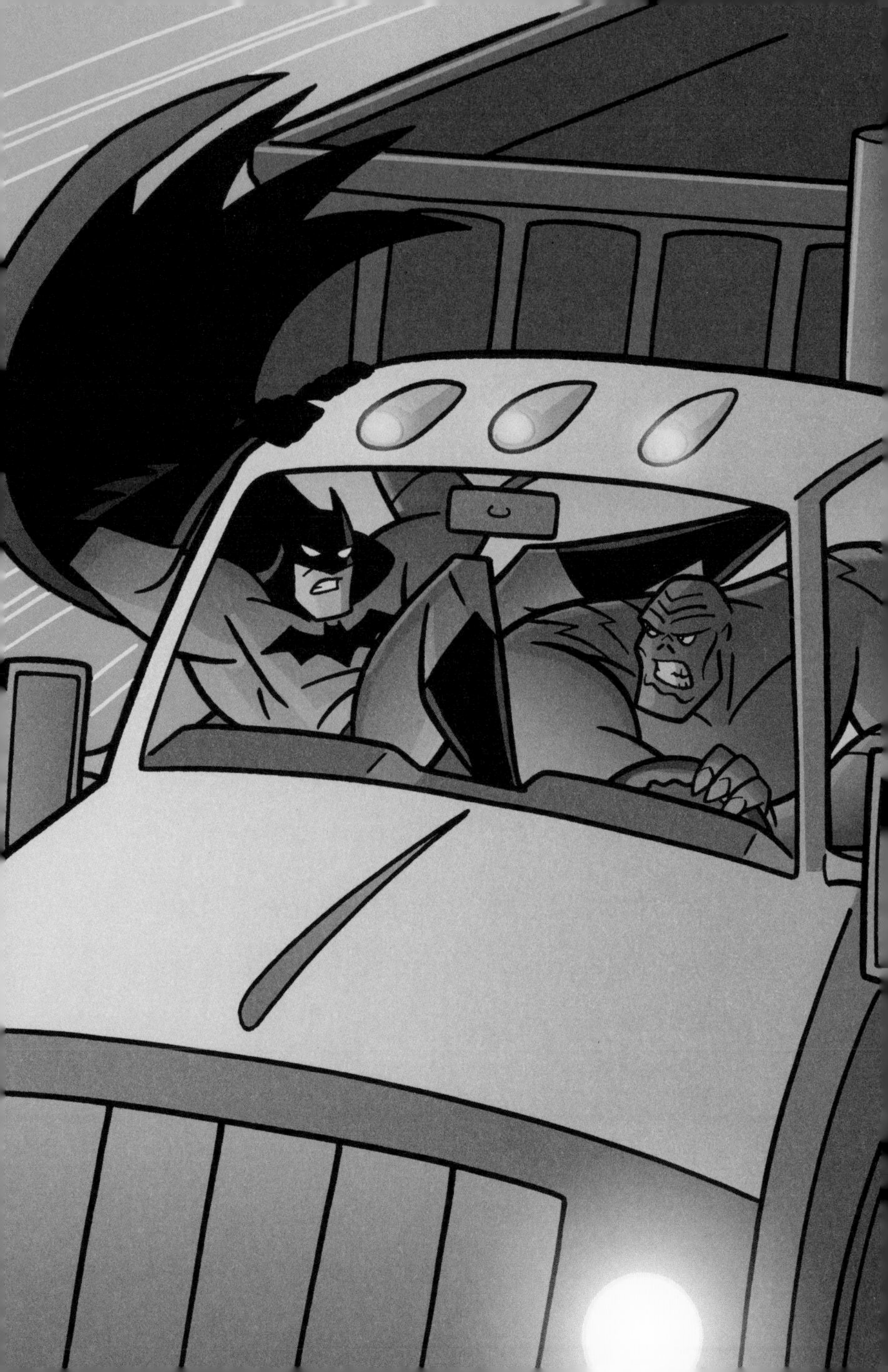

He knocked Croc right out of the dump truck. As Croc rolled onto the ground, Batman landed right next to him.

"I've had just about enough of you!" roared Croc. "I am done playing around. You're dead meat, Batman!"

Faster than Batman could move, Croc leaped to his feet and grabbed the Caped Crusader in a bear hug. Croc raised Batman above his head, and then smashed him into the ground. **SLAM!**

"Now, Kite Man!" shouted Batman.

Croc turned and saw Kite Man in the distance. He was flying a kite high in the moonlit sky.

"You've got to be kidding me," said Croc. He waved a clawed fist dismissively at Kite Man and turned back to Batman.

As Croc moved toward Batman to throw a punch, Kite Man guided his kite toward the green menace.

The scaly giant didn't try to swat the kite away. He didn't even bother to look at it. So he didn't see that it had one of Batman's tranquilizer Batarangs attached to it.

Kite Man flew it perfectly — right into the small soft spot in Croc's scaly armor.

"Arrggh!" said Croc as the kite-propelled Batarang hit him in the chest. He fell to his knees as the tranquilizer took immediate effect.

"I don't believe it," he cried. "I've been beaten by a stupid kite!" Croc toppled over and landed on his face. **THUD!**

Batman leaned over Croc. The green monster was snoring, sound asleep.

Before Batman could thank his strange partner, the wail of police cars filled the air.

"Sorry, Kite Man," Batman said. "But I'm afraid I can't let you go, even though you did help capture Killer Croc."

"Oh, that's okay," smiled Kite Man. "I *want* to go to jail!"

"Huh?" Batman said. He was puzzled by the criminal's strange confession.

"Wait until the other crooks hear that I'm the guy who brought down Killer Croc!" exclaimed Kite Man. "No one will ever call me silly again! The name Kite Man will finally get the respect it deserves!"

SKKKREEEEEEE A police van skidded to a stop. Officers rushed out and grabbed the groggy Croc. They lifted the villain into the van.

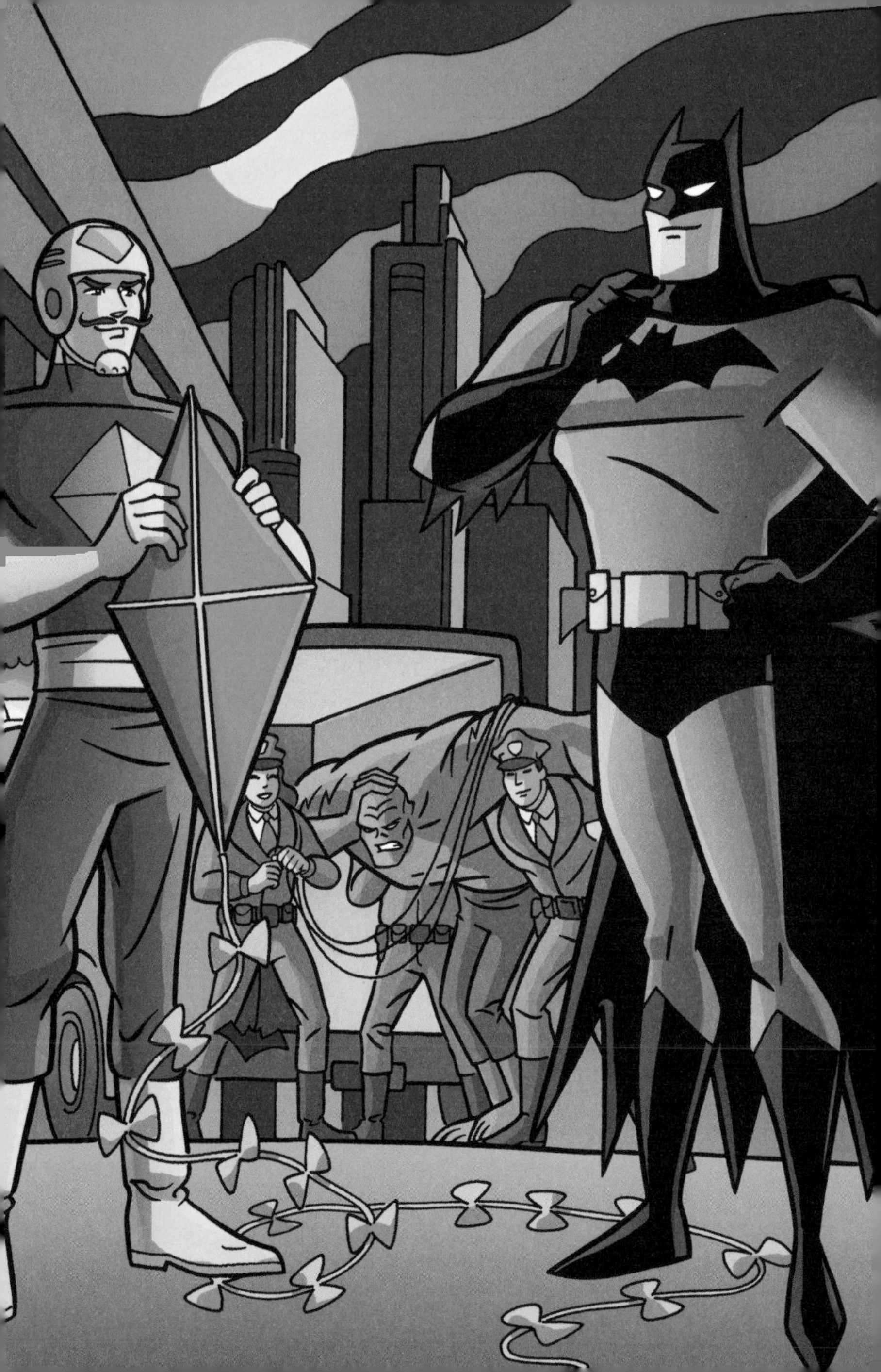

When they had loaded Croc into the police van, Kite Man strutted right up to them.

"Who wants to be the first to get the autograph of the toughest villain in Gotham?" he asked proudly as he hopped in the van. "That's right. I'm the crook who took down Killer Croc!"

The police looked at Batman, who simply shrugged. "He's more dangerous than he looks, fellas," said the Dark Knight.

The police closed the van's doors with both villains inside. Batman could still hear Kite Man bragging over the loud sirens.

Batman reached into his Utility Belt and grabbed his grapnel gun. **WHOOOOSH!** He shot it into the air, aiming at the roof of the Department of Transportation building.

As Batman soared through the air, he couldn't help but smile. *Tonight, I stopped one monster,* he thought, *but it looks like I may have created another!*

Killer Croc

REAL NAME: Waylon Jones

OCCUPATION: Professional Criminal

BASE: Gotham City's Sewers

HEIGHT:
7 feet 5 inches

WEIGHT:
686 pounds

EYES:
Red

HAIR:
None

Waylon Jones was born with a rare disease that made his skin scaly and green. Seen as a monster wherever he went, he decided to use his fearsome appearance to frighten his opponents as a professional wrestler. "Killer Croc" easily muscled his way through the ranks to become champion. After clobbering all of his opponents, Croc began to realize just how strong he really was. He decided to use that strength to his advantage. Soon, Killer Croc was feared throughout the criminal underworld — and climbed to the top of Batman's most wanted list.

G.C.P.D. GOTHAM CITY POLICE DEPARTMENT

- Croc has a skin disease called "epidermolytic hyperkeratosis." It has made his skin tough and scaly, protecting him from knives and bullets. It also makes him look like a crocodile.

- Croc once asked a scientist to cure him of his crocodile-like disease. When the treatment failed, he lost his temper and swallowed the scientist whole!

- With his razor-sharp claws and jagged teeth, Killer Croc is a dangerous super-villain. He has been known to give in to animal-like rages, making him extremely unpredictable and deadly.

- Kliller Croc has super-speed, super-strength, and fast healing powers. He can even regrow lost limbs, making it extremely difficult to put this vile villain down for the count.

CONFIDENTIAL

BIOGRAPHIES

Scott Sonneborn has written 20 books, one circus (for Ringling Bros. Barnum & Bailey), and a bunch of TV shows. He's been nominated for an Emmy, and he spent three very cool years working at DC Comics. He lives in Los Angeles with his wife and their two sons.

Erik Doescher is a freelance illustrator and video game designer based in Dallas, Texas. He attended the School of Visual Arts in New York City. Erik illustrated for a number of comic studios throughout the 1990s, and then moved to Texas to pursue videogame development and design. However, he has not completely given up on illustrating his favorite comic book characters.

Lee Loughridge has been working in comics for more than 14 years. He currently lives in sunny California in a tent on the beach.

Mike DeCarlo is a longtime contributor of comic art whose range extends from Batman and Iron Man to Bugs Bunny and Scooby-Doo. He resides in Connecticut with his wife and four children.

GLOSSARY

accessed (AK-sessd)—got information from a computer

attached (uh-TACHD)—joined or fixed together

collapsed (kuh-LAPSD)—fell down suddenly from weakness

dismissively (diss-MISS-iv-lee)—if you act dismissively, you indicate that something is not worth your time

fury (FYOO-ree)—violent anger or rage

groggy (GROG-ee)—sleepy or dizzy

pathetic (puh-THET-ik)—feeble or useless

quiver (KWIV-ur)—a case for arrows or other flying weapons

righteous (RYE-chuhss)—with good reason

shattered (SHAT-urd)—broke into tiny pieces

tranquilizer (TRANG-kwuh-lye-zer)—a drug that puts a person or animal to sleep

vintage (VIN-tij)—very good, or best of its kind

DISCUSSION QUESTIONS

1. Which one of the villains in this story was the silliest — Kite Man, Polka-Dot Man, or the Penny Plunderer? Why?

2. Batman and Kite Man manage to knock out Killer Croc with a tranquilizer. What are some other ways Batman could have defeated Croc?

3. Which illustration in this book was your favorite? Why?

WRITING PROMPTS

1. Create your own silly villain. What symbol does he or she use? What kinds of crimes does your villain commit? Write about it. Then draw a picture of your villain.

2. Killer Croc said he was helping Batman by clobbering other villains and stealing their loot. Do you think Croc was right? Is it ever okay to steal? Explain your answers.

3. Even though Kite Man was silly, he still managed to help Batman when the Dark Knight needed it most. Write about a time when you helped someone. Who did you help? What did you do?

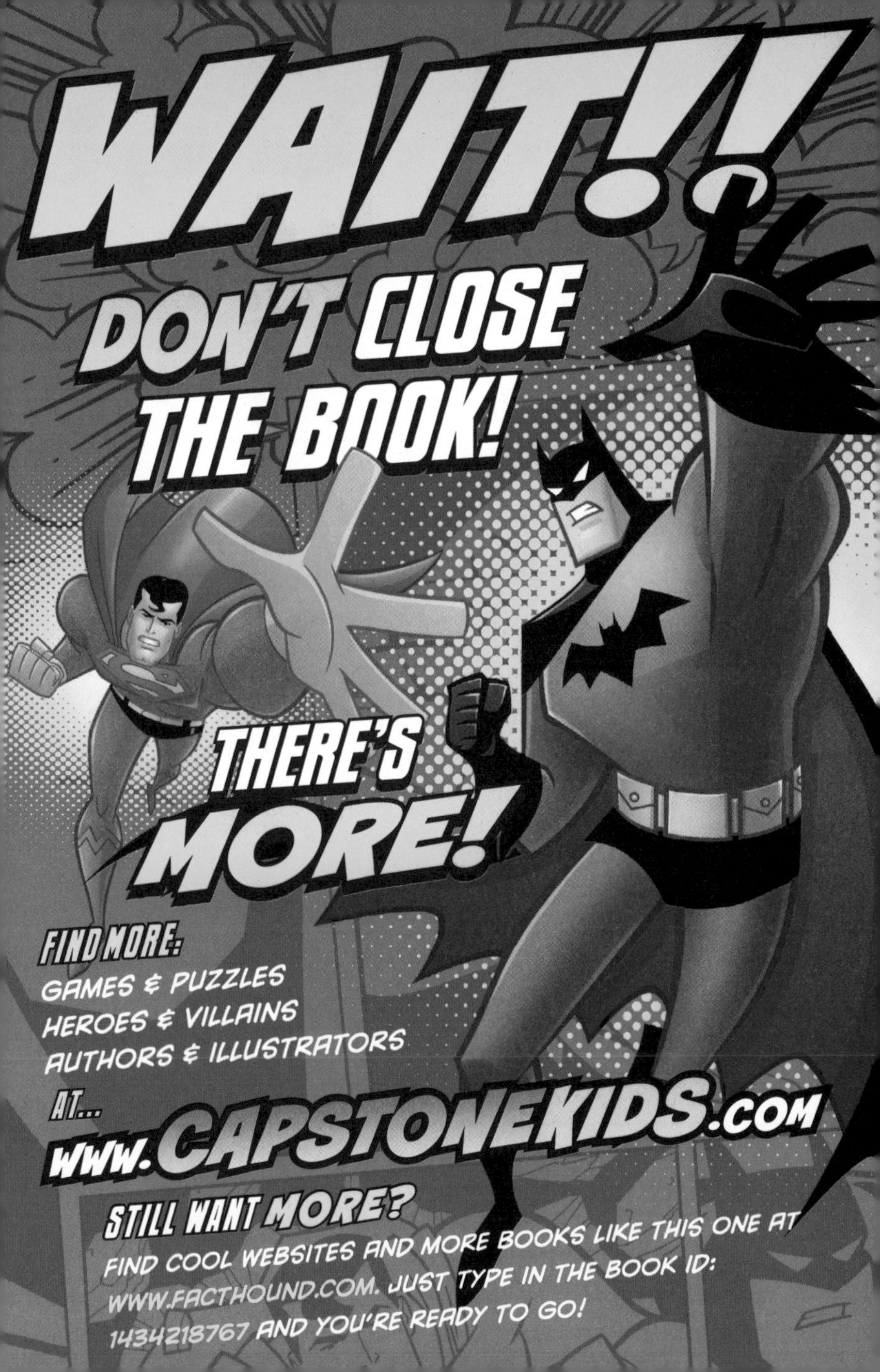
WAIT!!
DON'T CLOSE THE BOOK!
THERE'S MORE!
FIND MORE:
GAMES & PUZZLES
HEROES & VILLAINS
AUTHORS & ILLUSTRATORS
AT...
WWW.CAPSTONEKIDS.COM
STILL WANT MORE?
FIND COOL WEBSITES AND MORE BOOKS LIKE THIS ONE AT
WWW.FACTHOUND.COM. JUST TYPE IN THE BOOK ID:
1434218767 AND YOU'RE READY TO GO!

MORE NEW BATMAN ADVENTURES!

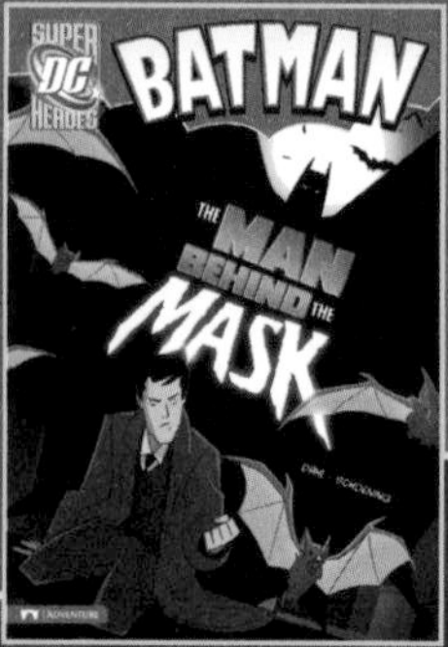
SUPER DC HEROES
BATMAN
THE MAN BEHIND THE MASK

THE MAN BEHIND THE MASK

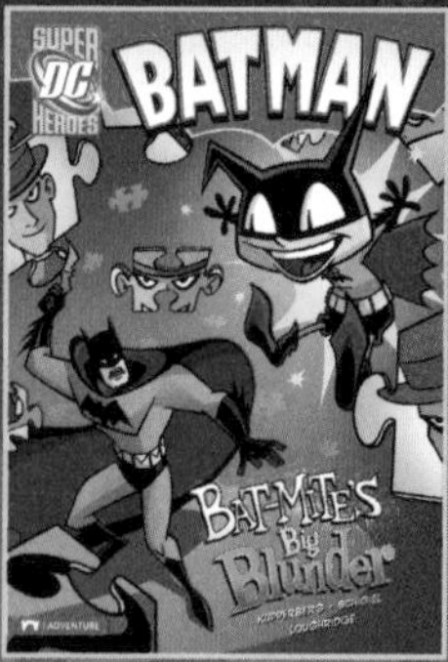
SUPER DC HEROES
BATMAN
BAT-MITE'S Big Blunder

BAT-MITE'S BIG BLUNDER

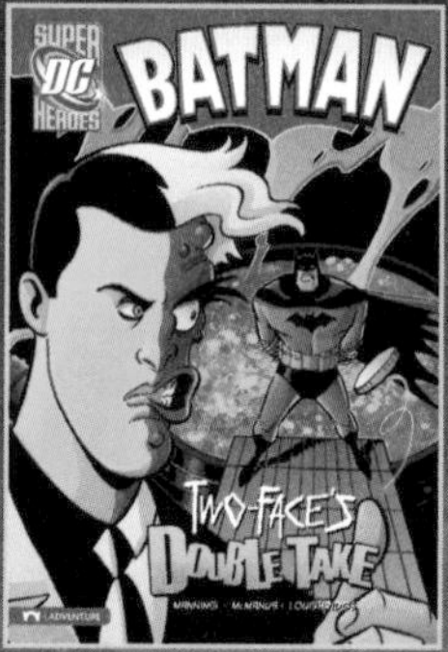
SUPER DC HEROES
BATMAN
TWO-FACE'S DOUBLE TAKE

TWO-FACE'S DOUBLE TAKE

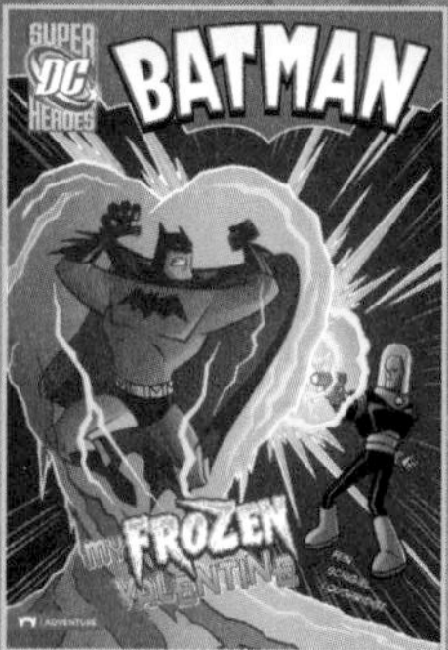
SUPER DC HEROES
BATMAN
MY FROZEN VALENTINE

MY FROZEN VALENTINE

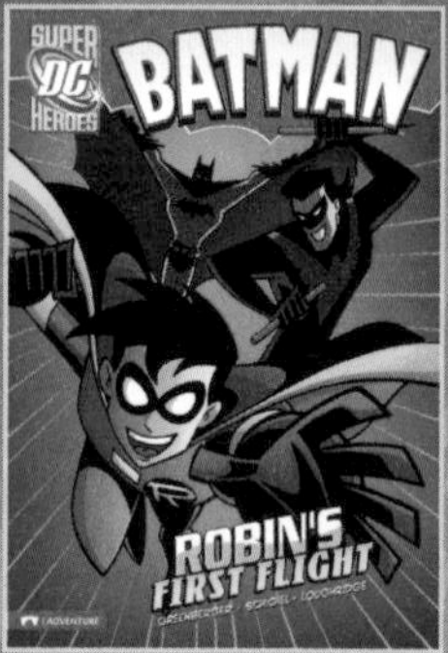
SUPER DC HEROES
BATMAN
ROBIN'S FIRST FLIGHT

ROBIN'S FIRST FLIGHT

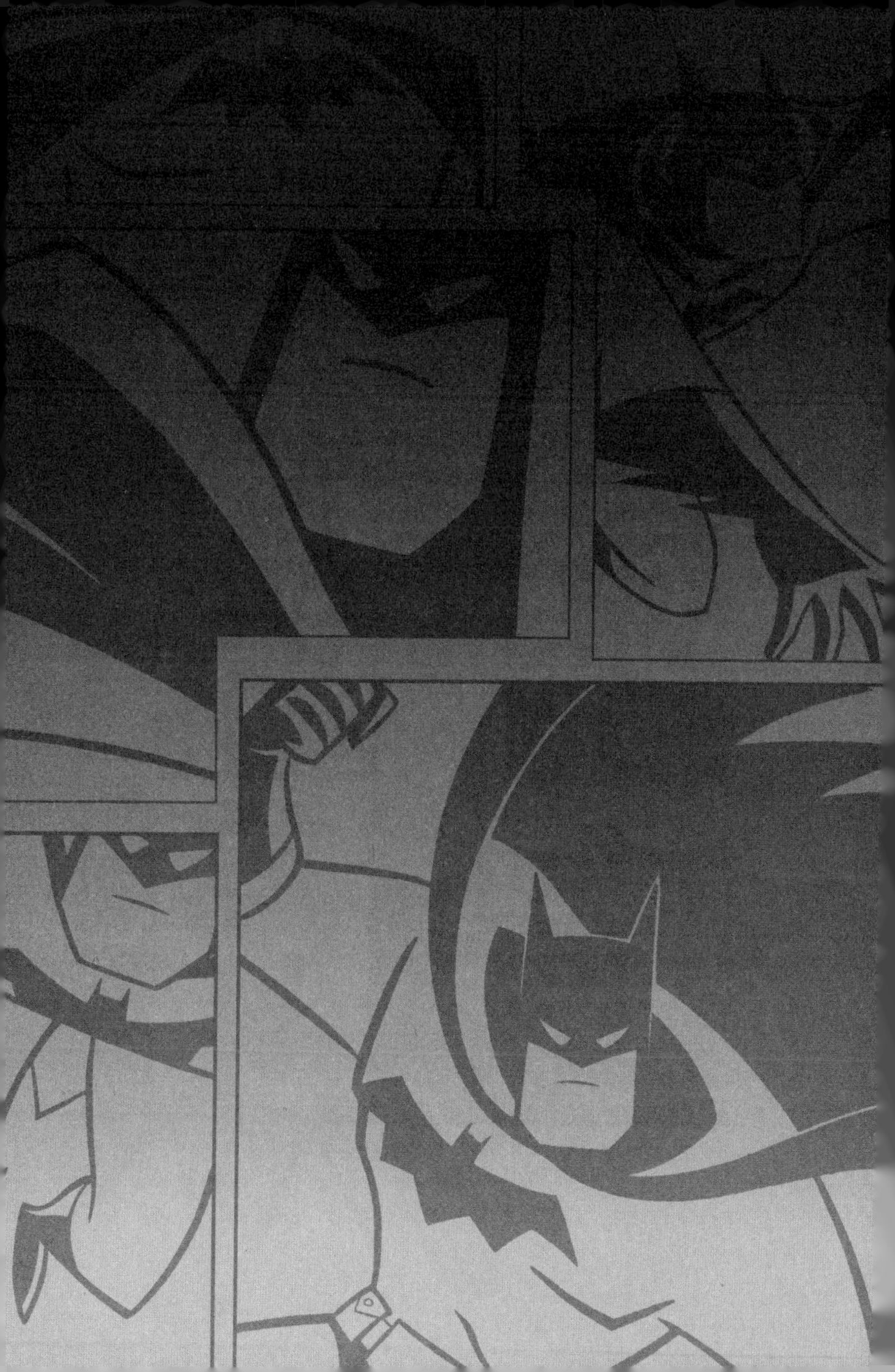

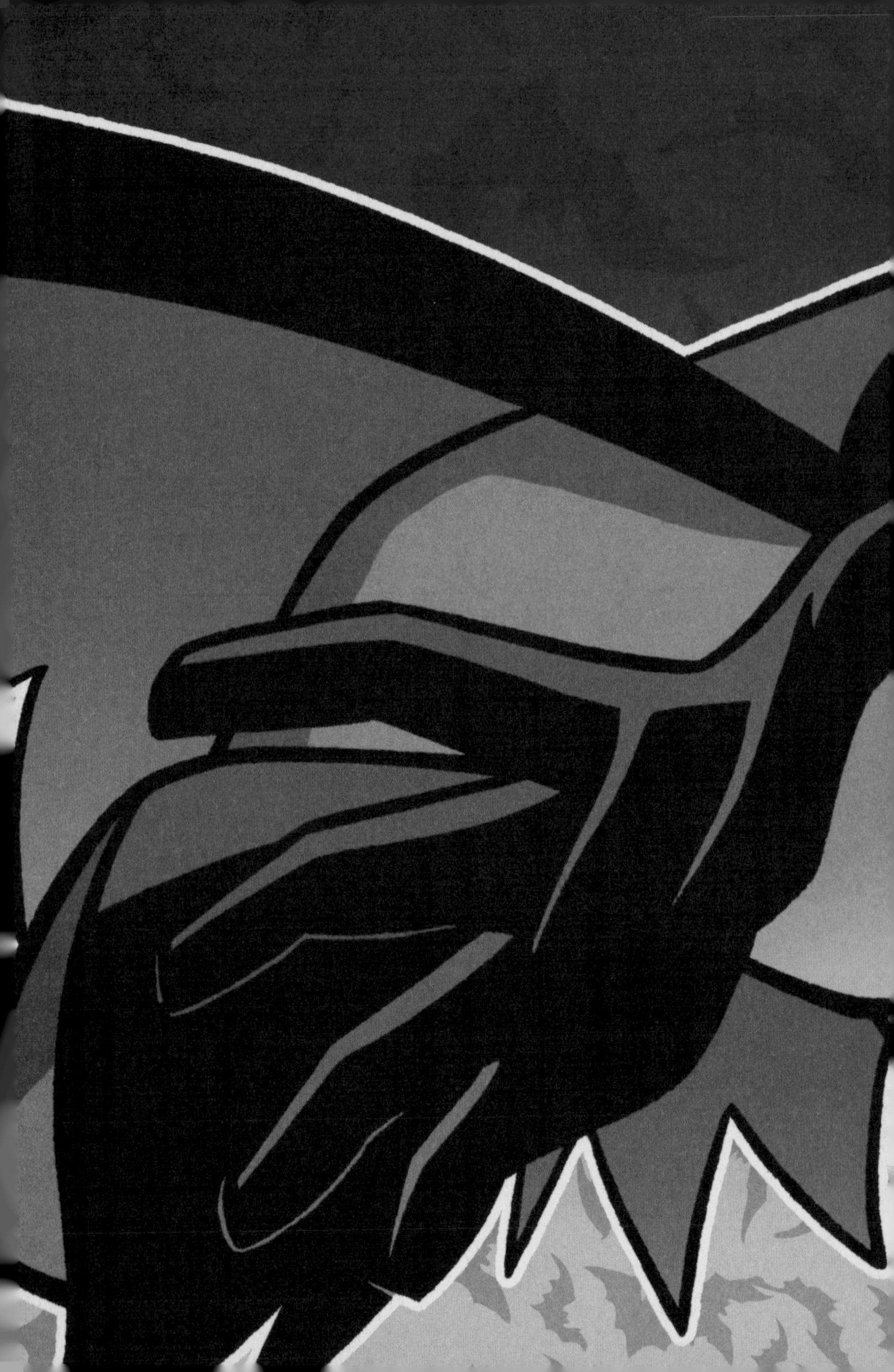

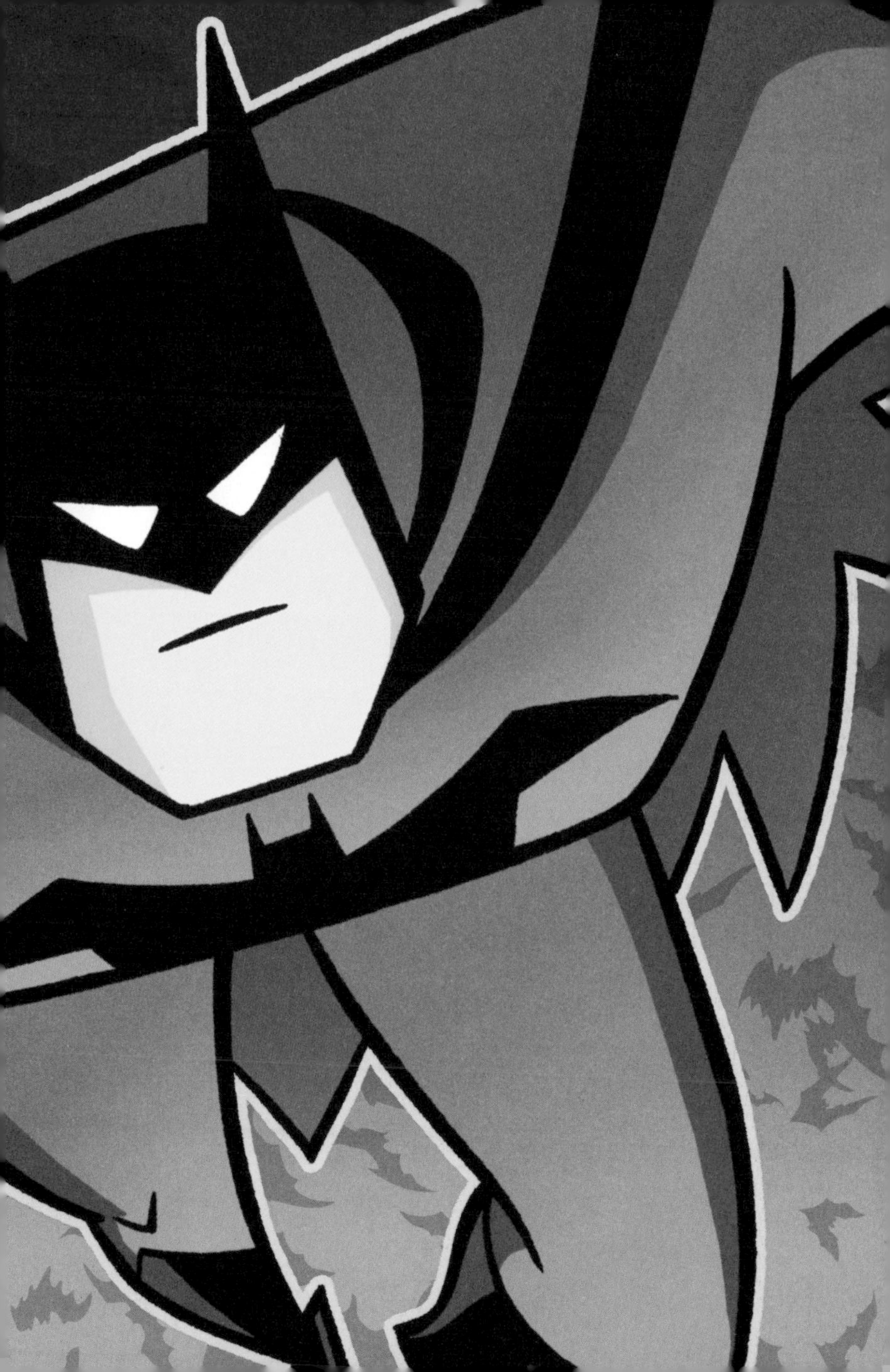

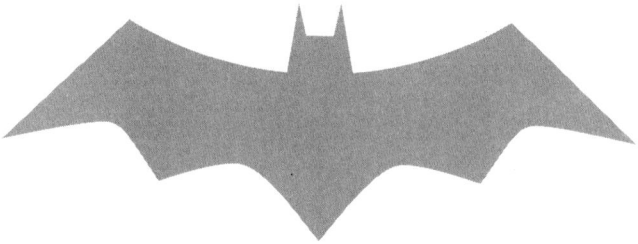